HEADLINES!™

SPORTS CONCUSSIONS

MARY-LANE KAMBERG

ROSEN
PUBLISHING®

New York

For Ann, Brock, Amy, and Skipper

Published in 2011 by The Rosen Publishing Group, Inc.
29 East 21st Street, New York, NY 10010

Library of Congress Cataloging-in-Publication Data

Kamberg, Mary-Lane, 1948–
Sports concussions / Mary-Lane Kamberg. — 1st ed.
    p. cm. — (Headlines!)
Includes bibliographical references and index.
ISBN 978-1-4488-1289-9 (lib. bdg.)
1. Brain—Concussion—Juvenile literature. 2. Head—Wounds and injuries—
Juvenile literature. 3. Sports injuries—Juvenile literature. I. Title.
RC394.C7K36 2011
617.4'81044—dc22

                                                                        2010017697

Manufactured in Malaysia

CPSIA Compliance Information: Batch #W11YA: For further information, contact Rosen Publishing, New York, New York, at 1-800-237-9932.

On the cover: A whack on the head in any sport can result in a concussion. Athletes in boxing, football, and other contact sports take the greatest risks.

CONTENTS

Two football players bump helmets. A basketball player falls and strikes his head on the court. A boxer is jabbed in the jaw. These athletes may experience a concussion. A concussion is a brain injury resulting from a head trauma, usually a blow to the head or a whiplash movement. With this injury, there is a temporary loss of normal brain function.

It's no secret that athletes are at risk. In fact, according to the Brain Injury Association of America, a concussion is the most common brain injury among athletes. The Centers for Disease Control and Prevention (CDC) says that about 3.8 million sports concussions happen in the United States each year. Some injuries are in the news. Others happen away from the spotlight.

University of Florida quarterback Tim Tebow had a widely publicized concussion in a September 2009 football game. The Heisman Trophy winner was sacked and hit his head. He lost consciousness and spent a night in the hospital. Travis Pastrana, the most successful racer in the X Games freestyle motocross, has had about twenty-five concussions.

Florida Gators quarterback Tim Tebow gets sacked in the January 2010 Allstate Sugar Bowl. Tebow suffered a concussion from a sack in a September 2009 game.

At least three of them have been severe. National Hockey League (NHL) star Eric Lindros sustained at least eight concussions during his career. Professional boxing champion Muhammad Ali has Parkinson's disease, which affects the central nervous system. Experts think that concussions may have contributed to his disease.

Former National Football League (NFL) players claim to have suffered long-term brain damage from concussions. The U.S. House of Representatives Judiciary Committee has held hearings about concussions. Research has helped to find ways to treat them. New guidelines for return-to-play have caused controversy. In short, sports concussions are in the headlines.

CHAPTER 1

A WHACK ON THE HEAD

T he recent surge in media interest in sports concussions dates to late 2006 and early 2007. In November 2006, the sports world was shocked by the suicide of Andre Waters, a former Philadelphia Eagles defensive back, at the age of forty-four. A January 2007 pathology report showed that the deceased player's brain tissue was damaged, probably from multiple concussions. Many began to suspect that concussions had led to Waters's poor mental health, and in turn, to his suicide.

A few weeks later, New England Patriots linebacker Ted Johnson announced that he had suffered long-term brain damage from concussions. He said a neurologist connected his history of concussions to his depression and substance abuse. Johnson said that on one occasion, his coach, Bill Belichick, pushed him to participate in a full-contact practice too soon after a concussion. Johnson had another concussion during that practice.

The revelations about Johnson and Waters were only the beginning. Other players told similar stories. Former players reported brain damage before the age of forty. While the NFL had formed a committee to focus on concussions as early as 1994, the league was slow to agree that sports concussions had long-term effects. However, in the last few years, studies of retired NFL players have begun to provide evidence.

Studying Brain Injury in the NFL

In 2007, the University of North Carolina's Center for the Study of Retired Athletes published the findings of a study. Researchers collected a health survey from 2,552 retired professional football players and then analyzed the data. The results were disturbing. When compared to the group of players that had not experienced concussions, the group of players that had experienced three or more concussions had three times the rate of depression.

Former New England Patriots linebacker Ted Johnson discusses the long-term brain damage he sustained from multiple concussions.

The center published a similar study in 2005. The study found that football players with a history of concussions had a 37 percent higher risk of developing Alzheimer's disease than other American men in the same age range. Alzheimer's disease affects memory and other brain functions. It is most common among the elderly. However, the research suggested that retired NFL players have a greater risk of getting Alzheimer's at a younger age.

NFL representatives responded by saying that the UNC studies had flaws. They pointed out that the research was based on player surveys, rather than hard scientific data. They argued that players' memories could be unreliable. They also said the results weren't determined fairly because the NFL Players Association, which advocates for players, helped to pay for the research. An NFL spokesperson said teams treated players with concussions appropriately.

In June 2007, the NFL's concussion committee—the Committee on Mild Traumatic Brain Injury (MTBI)—held a special meeting with NFL doctors and trainers from all teams. The league also began its own study of retired players and concussions.

NFL commissioner Roger Goodell announced some new policies and safety procedures in the spring and summer of 2007. First, any players who were knocked unconscious would be required to sit out for the rest of the game or practice. In the past, players were sometimes returned to the same game in which they had lost consciousness. The league also started a confidential hotline so that players and team doctors could report, or "blow the whistle," on coaches who pressured injured athletes to play before they were ready. The whistle-blowers would be able to keep their names secret.

Goodell announced another new procedure. As a part of preseason physical exams, teams would measure the normal brain functioning of all players. This information would help doctors and trainers in the event of a head injury. Doctors could compare the player's baseline test with tests after the head injury, giving doctors more information to help diagnose a concussion. After time passed, doctors could retest the player to help them decide whether the player was still injured or had recovered. Goodell also announced that the NFL would distribute pamphlets to all players to educate them about the signs and symptoms of a concussion.

THE 88 PLAN ASSISTS FORMER PLAYERS

In 2007, the NFL and the NFL Players Association established a fund to help pay the medical bills of former players with Alzheimer's disease and other forms of dementia. Alzheimer's and other brain diseases affect memory, thinking, language, judgment, and behavior. Treating and caring for patients can be expensive, particularly when the disease progresses and symptoms worsen. Players who qualify for the fund can receive up to $50,000 per year for home care and $88,000 per year for institutional care (care in a hospital, nursing home, or rehabilitation center). Sylvia Mackey, wife of former NFL tight end John Mackey, encouraged the league to start the program. John Mackey suffers from dementia. The fund is called the 88 Plan in honor of John Mackey's jersey number.

Tight end John Mackey, Baltimore Colts, 1970.

In September 2009, the NFL announced the early results of its own study. The early results seemed to agree with the UNC center's study. The research suggested that Alzheimer's disease and other memory problems happened nineteen times more often in former NFL players than it did in other American men of the same age. But the league said more information was needed. The study would take more time. Final results would take until 2012 or 2013 to be released.

CONGRESS GETS INVOLVED

In October 2009 and January 2010, the House Judiciary Committee held two hearings about football brain injuries. Representative Linda T. Sánchez, a member of the House Judiciary Committee, took a lead role in the hearings.

At the October 2009 meeting, Sánchez played a videotaped

In October 2009, retired NFL players like Merril Hoge *(right)* testified to the House Judiciary Committee about the severe effects of sports concussions on the brain.

interview with Dr. Ira Casson. He was the cochair of the NFL's concussion committee. He also had a lead role in the NFL's health study. In the video, Casson denied the health risks of concussions. Sánchez called Casson's assertions "ridiculous." The California Democrat said, "It sort of reminds me of the tobacco companies pre-1990s, when they kept saying no, there is no link between smoking and damage to your health."

After the October 2009 hearing, the players' union said Casson was the wrong person to lead the NFL research study. He had often disagreed with research results that linked concussions and long-term damage, saying they were wrong. The union thought he was not open-minded about the subject. It wanted him removed. Casson and his cochair, Dr. David Viano, stepped down in November.

On January 4, 2010, the House Judiciary Committee held a follow-up hearing about concussions. Linebacker Ted Johnson told his story. So did Kyle Turley, former NFL offensive lineman for the New Orleans Saints, St. Louis Rams, and Kansas City Chiefs. Turley talked about his headaches, dizzy spells, and other signs of brain damage.

The House Judiciary Committee questioned Casson directly at the second hearing. Casson repeated his position to the Judiciary Committee: in his opinion, there was not enough evidence to conclude that football concussions caused long-term brain damage in professional players. He said that more study was needed.

According to an article by Alan Schwartz in the *New York Times*, representatives of colleges, high schools, and youth football leagues talked about their programs at the January hearing. In addition, Turley and other NFL witnesses expressed their concern about concussions in scholastic and youth sports. Many head injuries occur in young players. However, unlike NFL games, most youth football games do not have doctors present.

Dr. David Klossner, the director of health and safety for the National Collegiate Athletic Association (NCAA), said the organization would soon consider a new rule. The rule would keep players who were knocked unconscious or who had experienced memory problems out of games or practices after concussions. The rule would apply even if the symptoms went away shortly after the injury.

Scott Hallenbeck, the executive director of USA Football, also spoke. His organization manages three million children who play youth tackle football. He said he would require all coaches within the organization to take a concussion awareness program. He also said that his organization recommended that medical professionals—not coaches—decide when an athlete is fit to return to play.

Changes Are Made

In December 2009, the NFL announced a number of new efforts related to sports concussions. The league offered to donate $1 million to a brain study at Boston University. Also, the league's committee on concussions began an investigation about helmet safety.

The NFL also changed the way teams decide when a player can return to the game. The 2007 rule barred an athlete from returning to play only if he had lost consciousness. According to the new guidelines, a player with any signs or symptoms of concussion would not be permitted to return to the same game. Also, teams now had to hire independent neurologists to give advice. That way, coaches and team doctors could not rush players back to work before they were ready. Players could be sure they had enough time for their brains to heal. The players' union agreed with the new rules.

The NFL's actions had immediate effects. Pittsburgh Steelers quarterback Ben Roethlisberger was one of the first players affected by the NFL's new rules. The league had announced its new policy in the middle of the season on December 1, 2009. Roethlisberger had sustained a concussion earlier that week. After that, he took several practices with the team. But he had headaches—a concussion symptom—after the practices, and on December 7, Roethlisberger had to sit out during a game against Oakland. In the same game, Steeler safety Ryan Mundy

Texas Tech University head football coach Mike Leach lost his job after a dispute about his treatment of a player with a concussion.

decked an Oakland wide receiver. In the past, referees might have considered it a good hit. But officials knew about the league's new emphasis on safety. They called a penalty against Mundy for unnecessary roughness.

Broadcasters began to change the way they described head injuries. For example, Daryl Johnston of the FOX network saw a player sustain a head injury in a game. He later said he was careful not to say "ding" or "got his bell rung." He didn't want to make the injury sound less serious than it was. Other game announcers stopped using words like "warrior" and "toughness." NBC Universal Sports stopped adding sound effects for hard hits in highlight films and promotions.

Colleges also took notice. Texas Tech University fired coach Mike Leach just before the 2010 Valero Alamo Bowl. The parents of the school's wide receiver, Adam James, filed a complaint about the way the coach treated their son after a concussion. A team athletic trainer said the coach told him to confine James in a dark equipment shed. James was not allowed to sit down in the room. Leach may have used such tactics to help his players "toughen up." However, in the new environment, his approach was criticized.

CHAPTER 2

INCREASING AWARENESS

The news about concussions in the NFL made players, coaches, and parents in all sports more aware of the dangers of the brain injury. Concussions typically come from falls, crashes with another player, or hits by an object. The injury can occur in any sport at any level—from youth sports to professional ones. High school sports with the most concussions include football, soccer, wrestling, and girls' basketball. The CDC, an agency of the federal Department of Health and Human Services, says sports-related concussions are increasing each year.

WHAT HAPPENS IN A CONCUSSION?

The brain is a soft organ. Its consistency is a lot like Jell-O. Usually, the brain floats in spinal fluid inside the skull, which protects the brain. If someone gets hit in the head, the skull absorbs some of the force—but not all of it. In a bad hit, the brain slams into the skull's inner wall. The soft tissue of the brain is hurt when it takes in the force of the blow. The blow can break blood vessels. It can stretch or tear nerve cells. It can even bruise the brain.

A concussion interrupts messages from the brain to the body. The injury also disrupts normal signals within the brain. That's why injured players may have confusion, impaired vision, slurred speech, or trouble

Blows to the head

A concussion occurs when a blow to the head results in the brain slamming against the skull. When a football player takes a hit, speeds range from 17-25 mph (27-40 kph).

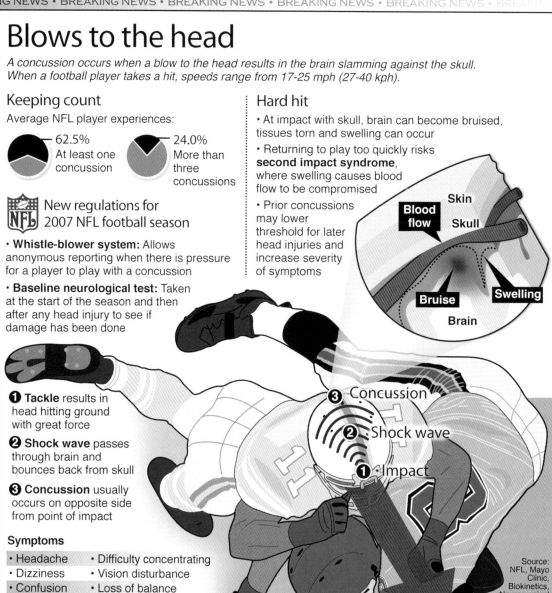

Keeping count

Average NFL player experiences:

62.5%
At least one concussion

24.0%
More than three concussions

New regulations for 2007 NFL football season

• **Whistle-blower system:** Allows anonymous reporting when there is pressure for a player to play with a concussion

• **Baseline neurological test:** Taken at the start of the season and then after any head injury to see if damage has been done

Hard hit

• At impact with skull, brain can become bruised, tissues torn and swelling can occur

• Returning to play too quickly risks **second impact syndrome**, where swelling causes blood flow to be compromised

• Prior concussions may lower threshold for later head injuries and increase severity of symptoms

Skin
Blood flow
Skull
Bruise
Swelling
Brain

❶ **Tackle** results in head hitting ground with great force

❷ **Shock wave** passes through brain and bounces back from skull

❸ **Concussion** usually occurs on opposite side from point of impact

❸ Concussion
❷ Shock wave
❶ Impact

Symptoms

• Headache	• Difficulty concentrating
• Dizziness	• Vision disturbance
• Confusion	• Loss of balance
• Ringing ears	• Memory loss
• Nausea	

Source: NFL, Mayo Clinic, Biokinetics, Neurosurgical Focus
Graphic: Melina Yingling

© 2007 MCT

In a concussion, a blow to the head typically causes the brain to slam into the skull on the opposite side of the impact.

with balance and muscle control. These problems may persist until the cells and tissues heal.

Each athlete has different signs and symptoms of concussion. A player with a concussion may have headaches, blurred vision, sensitivity to light, or ringing in the ears. The person may feel dazed or dizzy; he or she may feel sick to the stomach or vomit. The athlete may not remember the hit or what happened just before or after it. This memory loss is called amnesia, and it can be temporary or lasting. The player may feel weak, tired, or sleepy. He or she may have trouble concentrating or understanding information. The player may even lose consciousness. (However, an athlete does not have to lose consciousness to be diagnosed with a concussion.)

Dallas Cowboys quarterback Troy Aikman showed the symptom of confusion when he had a concussion during a 1994 play-off game. His helmet hit another player's knee. After the hit, Aikman thought he was playing a high school game in Henrietta, Oklahoma—not a professional game in Texas Stadium.

KEEPING THE INJURY SECRET

Sometimes it's hard to know if an athlete has had a concussion. Coaches often depend on what athletes tell them about their symptoms. However, in many sports players learn to play through pain. Coaches tell them to "suck it up" or "shake it off." In football, in particular, this is an honored tradition.

As a result, some athletes try to hide the injury. Some of them even lie about signs and symptoms that they have. They want to get back in the game. They don't want to let down teammates. They want to

Concussions in Girls and Boys: Is There a Difference?

Recent studies suggest that in sports that both girls and boys play, girls may have a higher risk of experiencing concussions. A study published in the *Journal of Athletic Training* in 2007 showed that girls in high school soccer sustain concussions 68 percent more often than boys do. A 2008 NCAA study found that female ice hockey players experience concussions more often than male players do.

Studies also indicate that girls and boys typically sustain concussions in different ways. Boys have more concussions due to player contact, and girls have more concussions from surface or ball contact. For girls, some of the most dangerous sports include soccer, basketball, cheerleading, lacrosse, and gymnastics.

There is also some evidence that girls' concussions are more severe than boys' concussions. Some experts believe biological differences, like different hormones or weaker neck muscles in girls, may play a role. Others wonder whether girls are simply more likely to report and describe their injuries truthfully.

keep starting positions. For professional athletes, fear of losing money or jobs may be a factor. But most often, athletes don't think the injury is serious.

In the book *Head Games*, former NFL quarterback Doug Flutie talked about why it is hard for players to know they have an injury. "When you get it, you feel fine," he said. "But thirty seconds later, you can't remember what happened."

Flutie said that even players who know they are hurt are often unwilling to report it. He added that many kids have the same competitive drive as professionals. Whether they are in the NFL or a youth league, athletes don't want to leave games and let down the team.

This "tough-guy" attitude should never apply to sports concussions. As former NFL quarterback Warren Moon stated in *Never Give Up on Your Dream*, "There were many games where I took a big hit, and 'boom,' I didn't feel right. It's about being honest with yourself. Football is important. But life is more important."

POST-CONCUSSION AND SECOND IMPACT SYNDROMES

The CDC says the number of sports-related concussions is increasing. Boys have more concussions from player contact, while girls have more concussions from ball or surface contact.

Not all brain damage occurs at the time of impact. Some signs and symptoms of concussion take hours or even days to appear. Even a mild injury can cause serious results and take a long time to heal. For example, the brain can swell. Swelling cuts off oxygen and blood flow to soft brain tissue. Blood vessels within or around the brain can be ruptured, and blood can leak into the injured area.

About 10 percent of people with concussions get post-concussion syndrome (PCS). A syndrome is a group of symptoms that together define a disease or condition. Post-concussion syndrome is a set of changes in memory, mood, and attention after a brain injury. A person

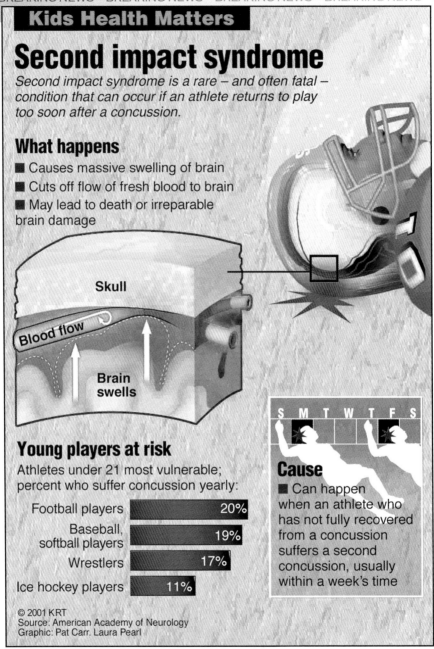

Kids Health Matters

Second impact syndrome

Second impact syndrome is a rare – and often fatal – condition that can occur if an athlete returns to play too soon after a concussion.

What happens
- Causes massive swelling of brain
- Cuts off flow of fresh blood to brain
- May lead to death or irreparable brain damage

Skull

Blood flow

Brain swells

Young players at risk
Athletes under 21 most vulnerable; percent who suffer concussion yearly:

Football players	20%
Baseball, softball players	19%
Wrestlers	17%
Ice hockey players	11%

Cause
- Can happen when an athlete who has not fully recovered from a concussion suffers a second concussion, usually within a week's time

© 2001 KRT
Source: American Academy of Neurology
Graphic: Pat Carr. Laura Pearl

An athlete with a concussion must take care to heal completely before returning to play, as another head injury could result in second impact syndrome.

with PCS may experience fatigue. Emotional changes, such as irritability and depression, can occur as well.

The most common symptoms of post-concussion syndrome are headaches and dizziness, which last for weeks or months. Some people find it hard to concentrate or read. Some have difficulty sleeping. Some may be grouchy or anxious. According to an article by Alan Schwartz in the *New York Times*, Hannah Stohler, a high school soccer player from West Hartford, Connecticut, had three concussions in one season. Afterward she had headaches. She also felt dizzy and suffered from depression ten months later.

One concussion can be dangerous. But recent studies suggest there is even more danger if the injured athlete returns to sports too soon. A player with a concussion who plays too soon can get hit again. A second injury before the first has healed can result in second impact syndrome (SIS). SIS can cause permanent brain damage or even death.

SIS is rare. However, most cases occur in athletes between the ages of twelve and eighteen. That is because teenagers' brains are still growing and developing. Concussions can cause more damage to young people than to adults. They can also take longer to heal in children and teens. Even if the second hit is mild, a young player can die from it if he or she has not recovered fully from the first injury.

Ryne Dougherty was a tragic example. The New Jersey high school junior sustained a concussion during football practice in September 2008. Less than four weeks later, he had a brain hemorrhage (a kind of stroke) while making a tackle in a game. He died two days later from bleeding in the brain.

SPREADING THE WORD

The Sports Concussion Institute says that 10 percent of all athletes who participate in contact sports have concussions each season. *Time* reports that high school football players alone suffer forty-three thousand to sixty-seven thousand concussions each year—and many more are unreported.

Since more information about sports concussions has come to light, several organizations have begun efforts to educate the public. Awareness campaigns include Brain Injury Awareness Month in March, sponsored by the Brain Injury Association of America (BIAA), and National Youth Sports Safety Month in April, sponsored by the National Youth Sports Safety Foundation (NYSSF).

The CDC has created a free tool kit for coaches, parents, and young athletes. The program is called Heads Up: Concussion in Youth Sports. The package contains free videos, posters, and educational materials. The information tells how to prevent concussions. It also explains how to recognize them and what to do when they happen. The material is available online at the CDC Web site (http://www.cdc.gov). In addition, the CDC has created a twenty-minute-long coaches' certification course about concussion safety.

The CDC has also made two short videos, which are available on YouTube. One is called "Keeping Quiet Can Keep You Out of the Game." It features a high school basketball player named Tracy, who had a concussion in a basketball game. She played a second game before the concussion healed and she passed out on the court. After that, she had to give up basketball. Tracy suffered from symptoms more than three years after the injury. In the video, Tracy helps young players understand that it is better to miss one game than to miss a whole season. In a second video, Tracy's mother talks about the effects of her daughter's concussions on the entire family.

The NFL created a public service announcement about concussions in sports. It began running during game broadcasts on the NFL Network in December 2009. The announcement used the slogan, "Help Take Head Injuries Out of Play." The commercial told athletes to take concussions seriously. It also told them to report symptoms, not hide them. It asked parents and coaches to learn the signs of the injury. The commercial also advised adults to get the approval of a health professional before letting young players return to play.

In 2008 the Sports Concussion Institute introduced Warren Moon as its national spokesperson for high school and youth football programs. The former Houston Oilers quarterback played more than twenty years of professional football in the NFL and the Canadian Football League. Today, he promotes safety, prevention, and recognition of concussions among athletes in high school and youth football programs. Moon had his first concussion at the age of eleven. He had six more during his NFL career.

DETECTIVE WORK

Why did news about sports concussions become such a hot topic? Most of the information we have about them is very new. In November 2007, Dr. Mark Lovell of the University of Pittsburgh Medical Center told the *PBS NewsHour*, "I don't think it's exaggerating to say that about 90 percent of what we know about concussion we've learned in the last five years."

Today, new tests and studies are being used to solve different parts of the sports concussion mystery. Lovell and Dr. Joseph Maroon created testing software to help athletes with concussions. Immediate Post-Concussion Assessment and Cognitive Testing (ImPACT) is used for preseason screening. Athletes take the test before the season begins. This is called a baseline test. It measures a person's brain activity before any injury has occurred. ImPACT measures twenty-one mental activities, including sight, memory, thinking, and reaction speed. If an athlete has a concussion, he or she takes the test again. The score helps doctors measure the player's recovery. Doctors use follow-up tests to guide treatment and to determine when a player can return to sports.

The NFL, as well as colleges and high schools, has used the ImPACT test. Other similar tests have been developed. They include CogState Sport, the Standardized Assessment of Concussion (SAC), and the HeadMinder Concussion Resolution Index (CRI). These tests provide important information about an athlete's condition. However, experts caution that test results should not be the only factor used to make return-to-play decisions. Pat LaFontaine, a former National Hockey League (NHL) center, once tested well after resting from a concussion. Even after the good result, he said he still felt like he was going to pass out. This symptom showed that his recovery was not yet complete. After sustaining multiple concussions and suffering from post-concussion syndrome, LaFontaine had to retire at the age of thirty-three.

Computerized tests like ImPACT score an athlete's mental functions before injury. After a concussion, athletic trainers can compare new scores to preinjury scores to measure how well the player's brain is healing.

STUDYING CONCUSSIONS' EFFECTS ON THE BRAIN

Athletes can have long-term or permanent problems after having multiple concussions. This is true even if the concussions are mild. In fact, some experts say that the total effect of having multiple concussions can be more significant than the severity of any one concussion.

The North Carolina and NFL studies seemed to connect long-term brain damage with repeated concussions. But another study

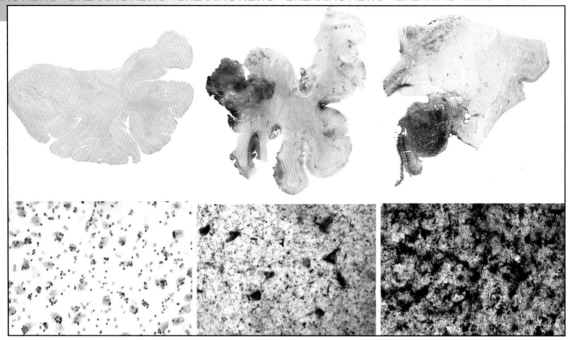

Tau protein appears dark brown in the whole brain tissue samples, above, and microscopic sections, below. The samples are from a healthy brain *(left)*, a professional football player *(middle)*, and a world champion boxer *(right)*.

begun at the Boston University School of Medicine in 2008 may provide even stronger evidence. The school's Center for the Study of Traumatic Encephalopathy (CSTE) is looking at brain and spinal cord tissue from former athletes who have died. Researchers hope to learn more about the effects of repetitive brain trauma on the human nervous system.

Many of the early examinations have revealed a brain problem called chronic traumatic encephalopathy (CTE). CTE is commonly found in boxers. Some have called CTE "punch-drunk syndrome." It affects emotions, behavior, and memory. It often results in attentional problems, memory loss, depression, anger, and lack of impulse control. The disease is progressive. In other words, it keeps getting worse over time. CTE is different from Alzheimer's disease, but it has similar effects on the brain. In CTE, a toxic protein called tau builds up in the brain. At first, tau interferes with brain activity. Later, it kills brain cells.

The first professional football player to be diagnosed with CTE was former Pittsburgh Steeler Mike Webster. The NFL Hall of Fame center died in 2002 at the age of fifty. The pathologist who examined his brain, Dr. Bennet Omalu, discovered a buildup of tau proteins. He concluded that the damage occurred over a period of time from repeated blows to the head. According to the *New York Times*, before he died Webster had serious psychological, physical, and legal problems. He was unemployed and in debt, and his marriage broke up. At times, he slept in his car. He eventually moved in with his son.

Since then, CSTE researchers, as well as other researchers around the country, have examined the brains and spinal cords of a number of deceased NFL players. Most of the tissue donors have showed signs of CTE. One of the football players whose brain tissue showed CTE was Andre Waters, the former Philadelphia Eagles defensive back who shot himself in 2006. The disease could have caused the severe depression that resulted in his suicide.

Houston Oilers linebacker John Grimsley had at least eight concussions during his NFL career. After he died, his brain also showed signs of CTE. During his later life, he had serious memory problems. For example, he had worked for months planning a big engagement party for his son. But the day before the party, he forgot all about it.

Other football players who were diagnosed with CTE after death include Tom McHale, Terry Long, and Justin Strzelczyk. However, the condition is not limited to boxers and football players. The brain of former professional wrestler Chris Benoit also showed signs of CTE.

CTSE is continuing its research and has started a brain donation registry. Athletes can agree to donate their brains and spinal cord tissue for research after they die. More than 150 athletes have pledged to donate. At least forty retired NFL players are on the list, including Ted Johnson. The first active NFL players to join the study were Matt Birk of the Baltimore Ravens, Lofa Tatupu of the Seattle Seahawks, and Sean Morey of the Arizona Cardinals.

Donors from other sports include Cindy Parlow and Keith Primeau. Parlow is a former soccer player on the U.S. Women's National Team. She has had two concussions and often has bad headaches. Primeau is a former NHL All-Star for the Philadelphia Flyers. Primeau retired from hockey in 2006 because of multiple concussions. Even simple training drills caused him to have headaches and feel "fuzzy." He has also had problems with balance and vision.

The players on the list will be interviewed each year during their lives. At death, their brain tissue will be examined. Researchers will see if there is a connection between injuries and symptoms during a person's life and signs of disease in the brain. Physical changes in the brain tissue can only be seen and studied after a patient's death.

Do Helmets Help?

Sports helmets have long been used to prevent head injury. Helmets help to cushion the skull. They absorb some of the shock from a hit to the head. Experts agree that helmets help prevent skull fractures. Also, the use of helmets cuts the rate of subdural hematoma. Subdural hematoma is a collection of blood on the brain's surface, usually from a severe head injury. However, how well helmets help prevent concussion is the subject of disagreement.

The NFL concussion committee began a study of football helmet standards in 2009. The study aims to learn exactly how helmets protect players. The study will also determine what qualities are required in a state-of-the-art football helmet and how to test helmets effectively. The league plans to share its results with helmet manufacturers.

Several organizations have established standards for helmet safety in a variety of sports, including:

- U.S. Consumer Product Safety Commission (CPSC)
- National Operating Committee for Sports and Athletic Equipment (NOCSAE)
- American Society of Testing and Materials (ASTM)
- European Committee for Standardization (CEN)
- Snell Memorial Foundation (Snell)

According to the *New York Times*, in recent years the standard procedure that has been used to test football helmet safety is the one developed by NOCSAE. The organization developed a drop test for helmets, which applies the amount of force that could cause a skull fracture. However, the drop test does not measure how well helmets protect players from smaller amounts of energy. Concussions often happen from milder forces.

Pittsburgh Steeler Limas Sweed gets fitted for a helmet for the 2008 season. The proper fit is important for maximum protection, but no helmet is concussion-proof.

The NFL has developed an additional test, which uses a plunger device to punch the helmet. Researchers can adjust the amount of force used in the hit. Again, some experts say the levels of force used are too high to determine whether a helmet protects a player from concussion.

NFL critics have questioned the league's ability to carry out the new helmet study impartially. They are concerned about relationships among committee members, the league's official helmet sponsor, and one of the testing labs. They say conflicts of interest among the parties involved could make the results unreliable. However, an NFL committee member said the critics should wait to pass judgment until the study is complete.

In any case, Chris Nowinski, president of the Sports Legacy Institute, says helmets will never fix the problem. He believes that even the newest helmet designs allow too much energy to reach the brain. In addition, he believes that providing advanced sports helmets might make athletes feel too protected and encourage more reckless play. He told the Judiciary Committee that some players use hard-shelled helmets as a weapon to increase contact with opposing team members.

Even officials at the top three American helmet manufacturers say that no helmet is concussion-proof. Dr. Robert Cantu, a board member of NOCSAE, agrees. He says that the only way to make helmets safer would be to make them bigger with more padding. But those helmets would be so heavy that they would likely cause neck injury.

Sports Helmets: Getting the Right Fit

Experts agree that to be effective, sports helmets, such as those used for cycling and skateboarding, must fit correctly. The helmet should feel comfortable. It should not slip around on the head. The head should not be able to move more than an inch sideways, up, or down inside the helmet. Further, the helmet should be impossible to pull off when the strap is in place. When the player lowers his or her jaw, the chin strap should tighten, and the top of the helmet should pull down a little. The helmet should cover the head evenly. It should cover the forehead and sit above the eyebrows. The player should be able to see without any part of the helmet getting in the way.

Heads-Up Soccer

Headgear has been allowed in soccer since the 2003 Women's World Cup and the 2004 Olympic Games. As of 2008, the U.S. Soccer Federation, NCAA, and National Federation of State High School Associations all allowed players to wear head protection. But experts disagree about whether headgear protects against concussion.

About 20 percent of head injuries in soccer are concussions, according to findings announced at the 2008 Masters of Pediatrics conference. Heading the ball is one cause. Another is forceful contact with other players. A number of experts worry that repeated hits to the head may result in damage from many mild concussions. Some experts think that soccer players should wear helmets. Others believe that wearing helmets will encourage soccer players to take greater risks.

In 2007, the *Journal of Athletic Training* published a study of women's soccer injuries in college games. The study found that heading the ball was not a main cause of concussion, but that player-to-player hits were. The International Federation of Association Football (FIFA), soccer's international governing body, sponsored another study. The study showed that headgear does little to protect against injury from heading the ball. However, the gear does have a benefit in head-to-head blows.

Also in 2007, a study of Canadian soccer players ages twelve to seventeen found that players who wore soft protective helmets had fewer concussions than those who did not. Those who wore the helmets had half as many injuries as those who wore no head protection.

Another piece of equipment believed to cushion the shock of a blow to the head is the mouth guard. Boxers have worn mouth guards since the early 1920s. Dentists also recommend them to protect teeth in contact sports like soccer, football, basketball, and hockey. Mouth guards cushion blows to the lower jaw. Some manufacturers say they help protect players from concussion. However, there is no research that conclusively shows that mouth guards lower the risk of concussion.

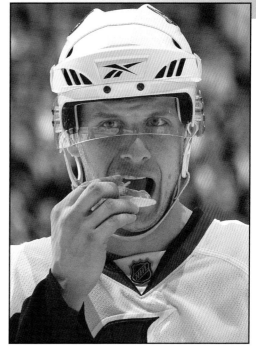

Athletes in sports like boxing, football, and ice hockey often wear mouth guards to protect their teeth and lower jaws. Studies have not confirmed that mouth guards prevent concussions.

CHAPTER 4

WHAT'S THE LATEST?

Today, when an athlete has a concussion, coaches are more likely to yell "Sit down!" than "Get back in the game!" Other developments include new ways to treat sports concussions and new advice about when players can return to play.

A NEW APPROACH TO TREATMENT

Sports medicine experts recently changed the way they diagnose and treat concussions. In the past, medical professionals treated athletes based on a rating of the seriousness of the injury.

The American Academy of Neurology (AAN) published its widely used guidelines for rating the injury in 1997. The system had three levels. Grade I was a mild concussion. The player did not lose consciousness, and any confusion or other symptoms lasted for less than fifteen minutes. Grade II was a moderate concussion. Again, athletes had no loss of consciousness. However, in this level of injury, symptoms lasted for more than fifteen minutes. Grade III concussions were severe. These concussions caused the athlete to lose consciousness, even if only for a brief period of time.

Each level had a different treatment plan. Many coaches and other adults thought mild concussions were OK. They thought that if the athlete was not knocked unconscious, he or she could get back in the game quickly. According to the 1997 AAN guidelines, athletes with a Grade I injury could return to play once they were free of symptoms for at least fifteen minutes. Grade II players had to be free of symptoms for a week before returning to play. Grade III concussions called for a trip to a hospital emergency room.

In 2009, the 3rd International Conference on Concussion in Sport issued a statement. The conference decided to abandon the grading scale. They recommended that health professionals base treatment on the condition of the individual athlete. They said that professionals should note which symptoms the athlete experiences and how long they last. The conference also emphasized that a detailed concussion history was important in creating a treatment plan for a patient. Finally, the conference encouraged use of preparticipation neurological testing. However, the statement warned that the computer tests should not be used alone; injured athletes should have complete medical interviews and examinations.

NEW GUIDELINES FOR YOUTH SPORTS

In 2009, an international group of neurologists updated its recommendations on concussion care for young players. Published in the *British Journal of Sports Medicine* in May 2009, the guidelines state that any player younger than nineteen who has had a head injury should never return to play the same day. Before that, the panel had said a player could return the same day if a doctor or athletic trainer cleared him or her. At first, the new statement caused controversy. But today, many sports programs at all levels have adopted practices that agree with the statement.

"When in doubt, sit them out" has become a motto for coaches in youth leagues as well as middle and high school sports to protect athletes from additional injury.

A number of states have passed new laws related to sports concussions at youth, middle school, and high school levels. The state of Washington, for instance, passed a new law in 2009. In Washington, any player younger than eighteen now needs a doctor's written approval before returning to play after a head injury. The motto for this law is, "When in doubt, sit them out."

The idea for the law came after an injury to a thirteen-year-old student named Zackery Lystedt. Lystedt had a concussion during a middle school football game in 2006. He returned to play. He then sustained another brain injury that put him into a coma for several months. He needed therapy to learn to eat and speak again. Jay Rodne was one of the state legislators who fought for the law. A few months after Washington's governor signed it, Rodne's eighth-grade son, Tye, sustained a concussion while wrestling. Tye Rodne was one of the first athletes who sat out under the new law.

State legislatures in California, Connecticut, Massachusetts, Maine, Missouri, New Jersey, Pennsylvania, and Rhode Island are also paying attention to the issue. These states' leaders are either studying the issue or drafting new laws.

The U.S. Congress is considering a bill that would create national guidelines about concussions in high school and youth sports. U.S. Representative Bill Pascrell Jr. of New Jersey has introduced the Concussion Treatment and Care Tools Act (ConTACT Act). If passed by Congress, the law would provide funding to develop and enforce concussion guidelines for children ages five to eighteen. It would provide money to schools and sports organizations for baseline testing and postinjury

SHARING INFORMATION

A number of organizations are working to share the latest information about sports concussions. In 2008, the 3rd International Conference on Concussion in Sport was held in Zurich, Switzerland. Organizers included the International Ice Hockey Federation, FIFA, the International Olympic Committee, and the International Rugby Board.

Also in 2008, the National Academy of Neuropsychology held its first sports concussion symposium. More than two hundred neuropsychologists and sports medicine professionals attended. Experts in sports concussion talked about the latest research and new ways to deal with concussions.

In 2010, the Sports Concussion Institute held its fourth annual National Summit on Concussion. Presenters discussed new discoveries about the biology of brain injury. They also offered information about treating concussion, such as what to do on the sidelines and at home after the injury.

U.S. Representative Bill Pascrell Jr. of New Jersey introduced the ConTACT Act to provide funding to protect young athletes from traumatic brain injuries.

testing. The law would also provide money to gather data about the incidence of concussions in youth sports. Representative Pascrell introduced the bill following the death of Ryne Dougherty of Montclair High School.

GETTING BACK IN THE GAME

Another new development is the wider use of computer testing in youth and amateur sports. In 2007, the California Interscholastic Federation asked one hundred thousand high school athletes in the state to take brain function tests such as ImPACT. The state of Hawaii also introduced high school testing. In addition, many sports organizations at all levels are beginning to rely on tests like ImPACT to guide treatment. They are also using a more careful method to decide when athletes with concussions can return to practice or play.

The main treatment for concussion is full rest until symptoms disappear—or until the athlete returns to preinjury test scores. For adult athletes, it often takes seven to ten days to recover from a mild concussion. In general, though, the younger the player, the longer it takes before he or she can go back to the sport. In children and teens, symptoms can last three weeks or more. A young, injured player should rest the body. He or she should also rest the mind. During the rest period, the player should not spend a lot of time reading, playing video games, or doing any other activities that challenge the brain (like doing math homework).

Once all signs of concussion are gone, the athlete should return to sports slowly. The Brain Injury Association of America recommends a step-by-step method to get the athlete back in the game. After each step, the player's mental and physical reactions should be tested. If symptoms come back, the athlete should return to the previous level of activity for twenty-four hours and then try the next step again.

The plan starts with light aerobic exercises. Aerobics are activities that use large muscles at low intensity for at least fifteen or twenty minutes. Jogging for twenty minutes, for example, is an aerobic activity. If no concussion symptoms reappear, the athlete can move on to exercises designed for the specific sport. Next, he or she adds

Young athletes take longer than adults to heal from concussions. Players who feel "foggy" take the longest to recover. Treatment includes rest and a gradual return to physical activity.

additional resistance—like weight training—to the workout. The athlete can then include noncontact training drills. The next steps are participating in full-contact practices and game play.

Researchers are looking for ways to predict which injuries take the longest to heal. The information can then be used to decide how much rest an athlete needs. Dr. Michael W. Collins studied high school football players in Pennsylvania. He found one way to tell which athletes would take the most time to heal. He said that players who said they felt "foggy" or felt like they were underwater took the longest to recover. Other signs of the need for a longer recovery period include trouble concentrating, vomiting, and dizziness.

CHAPTER 5

LOOKING AHEAD

How will news about concussions change sports? New research, laws, equipment, and technology can affect the ways athletes play games. What will new scientific studies reveal? How will new laws affect coaches' and players' actions? What new technologies will be created to address the concussion epidemic? No one can predict the future, but it's safe to say that sports concussions will stay in the headlines.

HEADING FOR MORE RESEARCH

Many areas are open to research. For example, future studies may focus on genetics. Does a person's DNA contribute to the risk of getting a concussion in the first place? Can genetics help predict the outcome or recovery time of a brain injury? To answer these questions, scientists will look for genetic markers that indicate an individual's tendency toward higher levels of specific biochemicals.

Research is also needed to learn about concussions in children younger than ten. Young children exhibit different symptoms from the ones seen in teens and adults. Their brains are less developed than those of older children, teens, or adults. Therefore, results of studies of older athletes may not apply to them. Gender differences also need

further investigation. Questions to explore include: Why is the rate of concussion higher in females than males? Why is there a difference in the severity of girls' injuries and the length of their recoveries?

New studies could also help determine which actions on the field pose the highest risks in a variety of sports. This knowledge would be useful for developing new rules of play or designing new protective equipment.

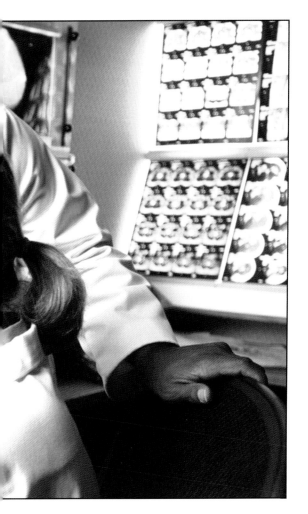

Future research about concussions may compare the brains of young children with those of teens and adults. Different levels of brain development may affect symptoms, treatment, and recovery time.

IMPROVING PROTECTIVE GEAR

Equipment issues will stay in the headlines. In football, both the NFL and helmet manufacturers are studying ways to design better head protection. In addition, the organization NOCSAE, which sets standards for athletic equipment, has proposed changes to the helmet impact test standard. Researchers may discover which levels of force cause the most danger to players. That information could contribute to new equipment requirements. The result may be improvements to football helmets.

On the other hand, evidence shows that some athletes play in a rougher way when they feel protected by headgear. Results of a study of Australian rules football (in which players are not required to

Future Trends and Developments

In the coming years, possible developments in the area of sports concussions may include:

- Changes in coaching style. Coaches may change their attitudes about playing through pain. They may be more careful about letting injured players play or practice.
- A change in attitude among players. With new understanding of the seriousness of the injury, players may learn to report concussion symptoms—not hide them.
- Quicker identification of concussion symptoms. Speedier identification of the injury may reduce the time needed for recovery. It might also reduce the number of players with long-lasting effects.
- Stricter enforcement of existing rules about player safety. With further education, referees may have a better understanding of rules that apply to player safety. Football referees at all levels have already shown greater attention to violations that injure players.
- Addition of game rules aimed at prevention. Sports with high rates of concussion may tighten old rules or pass new ones to make the sport safer. Research may determine which kinds of hits cause the most problems. New rules can address those on-field behaviors.
- Requirements to have medical personnel on-site at all athletic events. Sports organizations may be required to hire athletic trainers, who are trained in identifying signs and symptoms of concussions and making diagnoses and appropriate referrals to physicians.

wear helmets) showed fewer concussions than were found among helmet-wearing NFL players. Might the league decide not to use helmets at all?

New developments in soccer are likely to make headlines as well. Even though protective helmets are allowed in soccer, leagues have not stressed their use. That may change. Will more soccer players choose to wear helmets? Will soccer authorities encourage use of headgear? For now, leaders in the sport are waiting for more research about whether helmets help prevent concussion. Additional research might also determine which types of helmets work best.

Soccer players may resist the use of helmets. However, they also resisted the use of shin guards before they became widely used. If research supports helmets, players will be more likely to wear them.

The mouth guard debate will also continue. Manufacturers claim that mouth guards help to protect the mouth and jaw. However, research is needed to see whether mouth guards help prevent concussions. As studies reveal new information, recommendations for player protection will change at all levels of contact sports.

ENACTING NEW LAWS

Now that the U.S. Congress is involved in the sports concussion controversies, new laws may be on the way. If the ConTACT Act passes, new national guidelines for schools and other youth leagues will come into use.

Congress may take action in another way. As more studies connect concussions with long-term effects, the NFL may have to do more to deal with the issue of medical costs for players with lasting symptoms.

Congress might decide to require the NFL to pay. The league may also be the subject of legal action. Former players with health problems may sue the league for damages resulting from concussions they suffered during their careers.

High-tech football helmets are being tested in school sports programs in Maryland to see if the eighteen circular shock absorbers and snug fit help prevent concussions.

State and local governments and school boards may also take action. State legislatures govern school sports. More states could easily follow the lead of the states of Washington and Hawaii. They may enact new laws or adopt new rules and policies about concussions in high school and youth sports.

NEW TOOLS

Experts at the 3rd International Conference on Concussion in Sport developed a questionnaire called the Sport Concussion Assessment Tool (SCAT2). The athlete rates the severity of his or her symptoms. The assessment can be used to help evaluate head injury,

Boston Bruins center Marc Savard and General Manager Peter Chiarelli discussed the player's status after a March 2010 concussion. Savard missed eighteen regular season games and six play-off games.

measure recovery, and determine when an athlete can return to play. The tool is expected to gain wide use at all levels of sport. However, doctors should rely on it as only one part of the evidence they need.

New technology may soon improve diagnosis and treatment of sports concussions. The 2009 statement of agreement from Zurich said that brain scans are not yet helpful in diagnosing a concussion. However, some new imaging technology shows promise. Better tests that take pictures of the soft tissue of the brain are on the horizon. For example, improved magnetic resonance imaging (MRI) tests may soon show doctors the severity of concussions through their different patterns. They may also be used to measure how well an athlete is healing.

Interviews with athletes who have suffered from concussions continue to interest newspaper and broadcast reporters. Their stories will continue to raise awareness about concussions in sports. For example, many former boxers and football players have serious problems with CTE. As more cases come to light, there will likely be calls for leagues to reduce violence in these sports. Some people have even suggested that boxing and football be banned. There may be efforts to prohibit high-risk sports altogether.

Interest in concussion has already changed sports. Those who participate in athletics are taking steps to prevent injury. Parents, coaches, and medical staff are learning more. New methods to screen athletes are in use, and new policies affect the way injured players are treated. New guidelines for when players can return to practice or play are being enacted across the nation. Scientists are looking for more information. All of these developments help to protect athletes. And that will stay in the headlines.

GLOSSARY

aerobic exercise An activity that uses large muscles at low intensity over a relatively long period.

Alzheimer's disease A degenerative disease of the brain, commonly affecting the elderly. It results in memory loss, impaired thinking, disorientation, and changes in personality and mood.

amnesia A loss of memory.

athletic trainer An allied health care professional who specializes in the prevention, diagnosis, and treatment of injuries.

baseline test A test taken before injury occurs to use for comparison.

chronic traumatic encephalopathy (CTE) A progressive, degenerative disease of the brain found in people with a history of many concussions.

conflict of interest A conflict between one's private interests and one's public responsibilities.

consciousness The state of being conscious; awareness of one's own sensations, thoughts, and surroundings.

dementia A brain disorder that involves the deterioration of mental faculties, including memory, concentration, judgment, and planning.

fatigue Physical or mental weariness or exhaustion.

irritability Quick excitability to annoyance or anger.

magnetic resonance imaging (MRI) A medical test that takes pictures of soft tissue in the body.

neurological Relating to the science of the nervous system.

neurologist A doctor who is an expert in the brain and nervous system.

neuropsychologist A health care professional who is an expert in such brain functions as attention, language, and memory.

pathology The study of bodily changes that occur as a result of disease.

post-concussion syndrome (PCS) A disorder in which a combination of symptoms, such as headaches and dizziness, lasts for weeks or months after a concussion.

progressive Tending to become more severe over time.

second impact syndrome (SIS) A rare but serious condition caused by sustaining a second concussion before an earlier concussion has healed.

subdural hematoma A collection of blood on the brain's surface.

symposium A conference on a scholarly topic.

syndrome A group of symptoms that together define a disease or condition.

tau A toxic protein in the brain.

whistle-blower A person who reports violations of law or policy after witnessing them in the workplace.

FOR MORE INFORMATION

American Association of Neurological Surgeons

5550 Meadowbrook Drive

Rolling Meadows, IL 60008

(888) 566-2267

E-mail: info@aans.org

Web site: http://www.aans.org

The American Association of Neurological Surgeons is a scientific and
educational association dedicated to the treatment of neurological
disorders.

Brain Injury Association of America

1608 Spring Hill Road, Suite 110

Vienna, VA 22182

(800) 444-6443

Web site: http://www.biausa.org

The Brain Injury Association of America provides information, education, and support to people living with traumatic brain injury and
their families.

Brain Injury Association of Canada

155 Queen Street, Suite 808

Ottawa, ON K1P 6L1

Canada

(866) 977-2492

E-mail: info@biac-aclc.ca

Web site: http://www.biac-aclc.ca

The Brain Injury Association of Canada is a national charitable
organization that seeks to improve life for Canadians affected by
acquired brain injury. The organization also promotes prevention,
research, and education in partnership with other associations.

Canadian Athletic Therapists Association

1040 7th Avenue SW, Suite 402

Calgary, AB T2P 3G9

Canada

(403) 509-2282

E-mail: info@athletictherapy.org

Web site: http://www.athletictherapy.org

This nonprofit organization promotes quality care for active indi-
viduals through injury prevention, emergency services, and
rehabilitative techniques. It also creates and monitors professional
standards for the sports medicine community.

National Federation of State High School Associations

P.O. Box 690

Indianapolis, IN 46206

(317) 972-6900

Web site: http://www.nfhs.org

The National Federation of State High School Associations establishes consistent standards and rules for competition at the secondary level. It oversees sixteen high school sports, as well as other activities, in all fifty states and the District of Columbia.

Sports Concussion Institute

5230 Pacific Concourse Drive, Suite 300

Los Angeles, CA 90045

(310) 643-9595

E-mail: info@concussiontreatment.com

Web site: http://www.concussiontreatment.com

The Sports Concussion Institute's three clinics work to prevent, diagnose, and treat concussions. The Warren Moon/SCI prevention and intervention program serves high school and youth athletes, as well as families, schools, coaches, and medical personnel.

Sports Legacy Institute

230 Third Avenue

Waltham, MA 02451-7528

E-mail: info@sportslegacy.org

Web site: http://www.sportslegacy.org

The Sports Legacy Institute was founded to address the concussion crisis in sports and the military through medical research, treatment, and education and prevention. Its primary focus is the study of brain conditions caused by multiple concussions and other head injuries. It also seeks to educate coaches, athletes, and parents.

ThinkFirst National Injury Prevention Foundation

1801 N. Mill Street, Suite F

Naperville, IL 60563

(800) 844-6556

E-mail: thinkfirst@thinkfirst.org

Web site: http://www.thinkfirst.org

The ThinkFirst National Injury Prevention Foundation (formerly
known as the National Head and Spinal Cord Injury Prevention
Program) has developed a national educational program to help
prevent head and spinal cord injuries. It also addresses public policy
issues related to the topic.

USA Football

8300 Boone Boulevard, Suite 625

Vienna, VA 22182

(877) 536-6822

Web site: http://www.usafootball.com

USA Football is a nonprofit organization that serves as the national
governing body of youth, high school, and international amateur
football. It was endowed by the National Football League and the
National Football League Players Association in 2002.

U.S. National Athletic Trainers' Association

2952 Stemmons Freeway

Dallas, TX 75247

(214) 637-6282

Web site: http://www.nata.org

The National Athletic Trainers' Association is the professional association for certified athletic trainers. It seeks to improve the health care provided by its members and to advance the field.

WEB SITES

Due to the changing nature of Internet links, Rosen Publishing has developed an online list of Web sites related to the subject of this book. This site is updated regularly. Please use this link to access the list:

http://www.rosenlinks.com/hls/conc

Abraham, Philip. *Extreme Sports Stars* (Greatest Sports Heroes). New York, NY: Children's Press, 2007.

American Red Cross and the U.S. Olympic Committee. *Sport Safety Training: Injury Prevention and Care Handbook*. San Bruno, CA: StayWell, 2005.

Bellenir, Karen. *Sports Injuries Information for Teens: Health Tips About Acute, Traumatic, and Chronic Injuries in Adolescent Athletes* (Teen Health Series). Detroit, MI: Omnigraphics, 2008.

Bickerstaff, Linda. *Frequently Asked Questions About Concussions* (FAQ: Teen Life). New York, NY: Rosen Publishing, 2010.

Brodeur, Martin, and Damien Cox. *Brodeur: Beyond the Crease*. Missiagua, ON, Canada: John Wiley and Sons, 2007.

Doeden, Matt. *Sports Heroes and Legends: Doug Flutie*. Minneapolis, MN: Twenty-First Century Books, 2009.

Furgang, Kathy. *Frequently Asked Questions About Sports Injuries* (FAQ: Teen Life). New York, NY: Rosen Publishing, 2008.

Hughes, Pat. *Open Ice*. New York, NY: Laurel-Leaf Books, 2005.

Jandial, Rahul, Charles B. Newman, and Samuel A. Hughes. *100 Questions & Answers About Head and Brain Injuries* (100 Questions & Answers). Sudbury, MA: Jones and Bartlett Publishers, 2009.

Kane, Lawrence A., and Kris Wilder. *The Way to Black Belt*. Boston, MA: YMAA Publication Center, 2007.

Korman, Gordon. *Pop*. New York, NY: Balzer and Bray, 2009.

Marcovitz, Hal. *Brain Trauma* (Diseases and Disorders). Detroit, MI: Lucent Books, 2009.

McKenzie, Bob. *Hockey Dad: True Confessions of a (Crazy?) Hockey Parent*. Mississauga, ON, Canada: John Wiley and Sons, 2009.

Oliver, Greg, and Jon Waldman, eds. *Slam! Wrestling: Shocking Stories from the Squared Circle*. Toronto, ON, Canada: ECW Press, 2009.

Omalu, Bennet. *Play Hard, Die Young: Football Dementia, Depression, and Death*. Lodi, CA: Neo-Forenxis Books, 2008.

Thygerson, Alton L. *Sports First Aid and Injury Prevention*. Sudbury, MA: Jones and Bartlett Publishers, 2008.

Truman, Phil. *Game: Some Have It, Some Don't*. Mustang, OK: Tate Publishing, 2007.

BIBLIOGRAPHY

Albergotti, Reed, and Shirley S. Wang. "Is It Time to Retire the Football Helmet?" *Wall Street Journal*, November 11, 2009. Retrieved December 11, 2009 (http://online.wsj.com/article/SB10 001424052748704402404574527881984299454.html).

Brody, Cheryl. "Heads Up! Girls Are More Susceptible to Concussions Than Guys." *CosmoGirl!*, September 2008, p. 100.

Duff, Melissa. "Management of Sports-Related Concussion in Children and Adolescents." *The ASHA Leader Online*, July 14, 2009. Retrieved January 10, 2010 (http://www.asha.org/Publications/leader/2009/090714/f090714a.htm).

Epstein, David. "Football's Big Headache." *Sports Illustrated*, October 27, 2008, p. 18.

FoxNews.com. "All Clear? Head Injuries Get Attention from States." January 28, 2010. Retrieved January 30, 2010 (http://www.foxnews.com/story/0,2933,584130,00.html).

International Medical News Group. "Delay Return to Play a Day After Concussion." *Family Practice News*, Vol. 39, No. 7, April 1, 2009, p. 32.

McCrea, Michael A. *Mild Traumatic Brain Injury and Post-Concussion Syndrome: The New Evidence Base for Diagnosis and Treatment* (Oxford Workshop Series). New York, NY: Oxford University Press, 2007.

Moon, Warren, and Don Yeager. *Never Give Up on Your Dream: My Journey*. Cambridge, MA: Da Capo Press, 2009.

Nowinski, Christopher. *Head Games: Football's Concussion Crisis from the NFL to Youth Leagues*. East Bridgewater, MA: Drummond Publishing Group, 2007.

Quinn, Elizabeth. "How to Choose and Fit a Helmet for Sports." About.com, August 5, 2009. Retrieved January 5, 2010 (http://sportsmedicine.about.com/od/equipment/a/Helmets.htm).

Schwarz, Alan. "Dementia Risk Seen in Players in NFL Study." *New York Times*, September 29, 2009. Retrieved January 10, 2010 (http://www.nytimes.com/2009/09/30/sports/football/30dementia.html?scp=1&sq=dementia+risk+seen+in+players&st=nyt).

Schwarz, Alan. "New Guidelines on Young Athletes' Concussions Stir Controversy." *New York Times*, June 7, 2009. Retrieved January 10, 2010 (http://www.nytimes.com/2009/06/08/sports/08concussions.html).

Schwarz, Alan. "12 Athletes Leaving Brains to Concussion Study." *New York Times*, September 24, 2008. Retrieved January 10, 2010 (http://query.nytimes.com/gst/fullpage.html?res=9C03E7DB153DF937A1575AC0A96E9C8B63).

Shea, Joshua. "More Than Just Tooth Protection." *Sporting Goods Dealer*, November/December 2006, p. 26.

Slobounov, Semyon, and Wayne Sebastianelli. *Foundations of Sport-Related Brain Injuries*. New York, NY: Springer, 2006.

Solomon, Gary S., Karen M. Johnston, and Mark R. Lovell. *The Heads-Up on Sport Concussion*. Champaign, IL: Human Kinetics, 2006.

Sports Concussion Institute. "Concussion FAQs." 2008. Retrieved February 15, 2010 (http://www.concussiontreatment.com/concussionfaqs.html).

Sports Concussion Institute. "Resources: Warren Moon/SCI Initiative." 2008. Retrieved February 15, 2010 (http://www.concussiontreatment.com/resources.html).

Tenorio, Paul. "Congress Seeks to Reduce Head Injuries in Youth Sports." *Washington Post*, December 16, 2009.

Walker, Brad. *The Anatomy of Sports Injuries*. Berkeley, CA: North Atlantic Books, 2007.

About the Author

Mary-Lane Kamberg is a professional writer who has written extensively about health and sports medicine topics for *Current Health 1*, *Current Health 2*, *Healthy Kids*, *Kansas City Business Journal*, *Kansas City Parent*, *Kansas City Magazine*, *KC Sports and Fitness*, and *Your Health and Safety*. She coaches the Kansas City Blazers swimming team.

Photo Credits

Cover © www.istockphoto.com/dswebb; pp. 4-5 Kevin C. Cox/ Getty Images; pp. 8, 25, 38, 46–47 © AP Images; p. 10 Tony Tomsic/ Getty Images; p. 11 Chip Somodevilla/Getty Images; p. 14 Ronald Martinez/Getty Images; p. 16 MCT/Newscom; p. 19 Shutterstock. com; p. 20 KRT/Newscom; p. 26 The Boston University Center for the Study of Traumatic Encephalopathy (CSTE); p. 30 Michael Fabus/Getty Images; p. 33 Graig Abel/National Hockey League/ Getty Images; p. 36 Rita Rivera/Workbook Stock/Getty Images; p. 40 PNC/Brand X Pictures/Getty Images; pp. 42–43 John Foxx/ Stockbyte/Thinkstock; p. 48 Brian Babineau/National Hockey League/Getty Images; interior graphics © www.istockphoto.com/ Chad Anderson (globe), © www.istockphoto.com/ymgerman (map), © www.istockphoto.com/Brett Lamb (satellite dish).

Designer: Les Kanturek; Editor: Andrea Sclarow;
Photo Researcher: Karen Huang